指挥俑　汉
高 56 厘米

Commander terracotta figurine
Height 56cm
discovered in Han tomb of Yanjiawan of Xian Yang

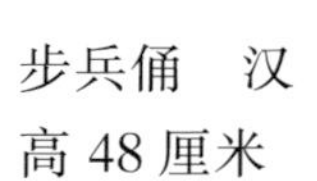

步兵俑　汉
高 48 厘米

Infantry figurine
Height 48cm
discovered in Han tomb of Yanjiawan of Xian Yang

背箭囊步兵俑　汉
高 48.5 厘米

Infantry figurine carrying arrow sack
Height 48.5cm
discovered in Han tomb of Yanjiawan of Xian Yang

战袍俑　汉
高 48～53 厘米

Terracotta figurine dressing in martial robe
Height 48cm
discovered in Han tomb of Yanjiawan of Xian Yang

步兵俑　汉
高 49.5 厘米

Infantry figurine
Height 49.5cm
discovered in Han tomb of Yanjiawan of Xian Yang

执盾俑　汉
高 48 厘米

Terracotta figurine holding shield
Height 48cm
discovered in Han tomb of Yanjiawan of Xian Yang

铠甲俑　汉
高 48.5 厘米

Terracotta figurine dressing in amour
Height 48.5cm
discovered in Han tomb of Yanjiawan of Xian Yang

簿书俑　汉
高 48.2 厘米

Official terracotta figurine
Height 48.2cm
discovered in Han tomb of Yanjiawan of Xian Yang

骑兵俑　汉
高 68 厘米

Cavalryman terracotta figurine
Height 68cm
discovered in Han tomb of Yanjiawan of Xian Yang

骑兵俑　汉
高 50～68 厘米

Cavalryman terracotta figurine
Height 50cm
discovered in Han tomb of Yanjiawan of Xian Yang